More Than Anything Else

story by Marie Bradby · pictures by Chris K. Soentpiet

ORCHARD BOOKS NEW YORK
An Imprint of Scholastic Inc.

Library of Congress Cataloging-in-Publication Data
Bradby, Marie. More than anything else / story by Marie Bradby ; pictures by Chris K. Soentpiet.
p.   cm.   "A Richard Jackson book." Summary: Nine-year-old Booker works with his father and brother at the saltworks
but dreams of the day when he'll be able to read. ISBN 0-531-09464-2.—ISBN 0-531-08764-6 (lib. bdg.) 1. Salt workers—
Fiction [1. Washington, Booker T., 1856-1915—Fiction. 2. Afro-Americans—Fiction. 3. Books and reading—Fiction.]
I. Soentpiet, Chris K., ill. II. T``itle. PZ7.B7175Mo   1995   [E]—dc20 94-48804

Printed in Mexico   49
Book design by Jean Krulis
The text of this book is set in 14 point Veljovic Medium. The illustrations are watercolor reproduced in full color.
20 19 18 17 16 15 14 13 12 11 10

To my Hampton Institute history teacher, Miss Alice Davis; my first-grade teacher, Mrs. Marie Boyd; and to my loving husband, Welby, and our son, Dennis —M.B.

Thanks to the towns of Malden and Charleston, West Virginia, and Ranger Haynes at the Booker T. Washington National Monument, Hardy, Virginia; also to Martha and Llewellyn Cole, Mrs. Seabolt, the Johnsons, Chris, and Richard Jackson—C.K.S.

*B*efore light—while the stars still twinkle—Papa, my brother John, and I leave our cabin and take the main road out of town, headed to work.

The road hugs the ridge between the Kanawha River and the mountain. We travel it by lantern. My stomach rumbles, for we had no morning meal. But it isn't really a meal I want, though I would not turn one down.

More than anything else, I want to learn to read.

But for now, I must work. From sunup to sundown, we pack salt in barrels at the saltworks.

A white mountain of salt rises above Papa's head. All day long we shovel it, but it refuses to grow smaller.

We stop only to grab a bite—sweet potatoes and corn cakes that Papa has brought along in his coat pocket. As I eat every crumb of my meal, I stare at the white mountain. Salt is heavy and rough. The shiny white crystals leave cuts on your hands, your arms, your legs, the soles of your feet.

My arms ache from lifting the shovel, but I do not think about the pain there. I think about the hunger still in my head— reading. I have seen some people—young and old—do it. I am nine years old and I know, if I had a chance, I could do it, too.

I think there is a secret in those books.

In the chill of the evening, I follow Papa and John back up the road, stopping to catch a frog. The frog wiggles and slips, but I

There is something different about this place where we live now.
All people are free to go where they want and do what they can.
Book learning swims freely around in my head and I hold it long
as I want.

Back in town, coal miners, river men, loggers, and coopers
gather on the corner. They are worn-out as me, but full of tales.

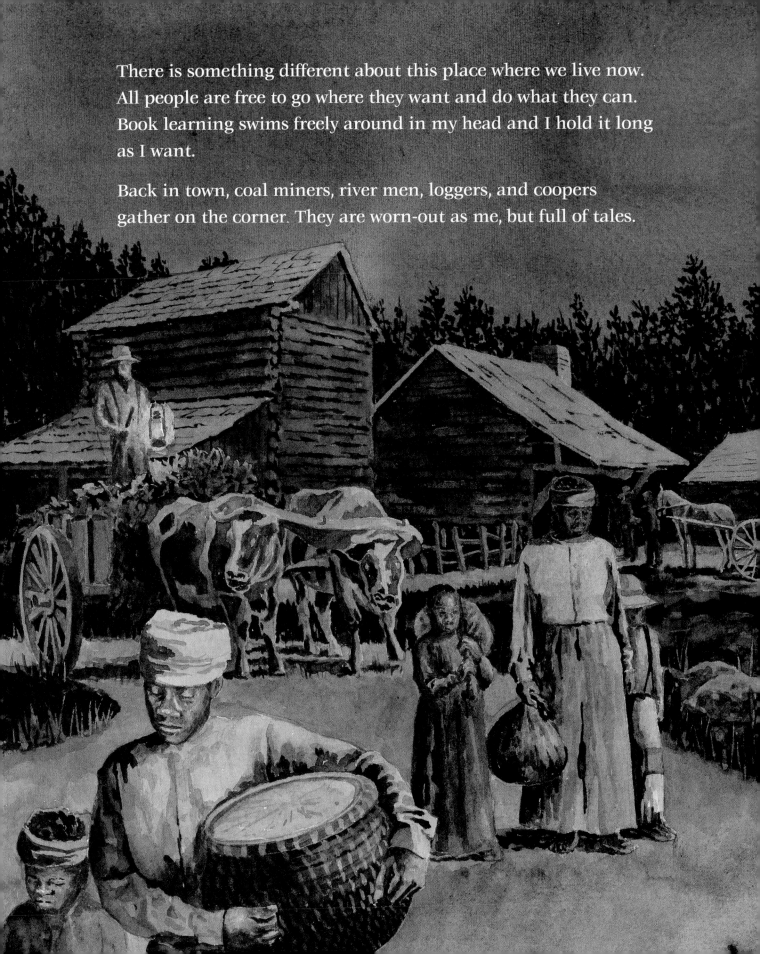

I see a man reading a newspaper aloud and all doubt falls away.
I have found hope, and it is as brown as me.

I see myself the man. And as I watch his eyes move across the
paper, it is as if *I* know what the black marks mean, as if *I* am
reading. As if everyone is listening to *me*. And I hold that
thought in my hands.

I will work until I am the best reader in the county. Children will crowd around me, and I will teach *them* to read.

But Papa taps me on the shoulder. "Come on." And John tugs at my shirt. They don't see what I see. They don't see what I can be.

We hurry home. "Mama, I have to learn to read," I say. She holds my hand and feels my hunger racing fast as my heart.

It is a small book—a blue the color of midnight. She gives it to me one evening in the corner of our cabin, pulling it from under the clothes that she washes and irons to make a little money.

She doesn't say where she got it. She can't read it herself. But she knows this is something called the alphabet. She thinks it is a sing-y kind of thing. A song on paper.

After work, even though my shoulders still ache and my legs are stained with salt, I study my book. I stare at the marks and try to imagine their song.

I draw the marks on the dirt floor and try to figure out what sounds they make, what story their picture tells.

But sometimes I feel I am trying to jump without legs. And my thoughts get slippery, and I can't keep up with what I want to be, and how good I will feel when I learn this magic, and how people will look up to me.

I can't catch the tune of what I see. I get a salt-shoveling pain and feel my dreams are slipping away.

I have got to find him—that newspaper man.

I look everywhere.

Finally, I find that brown face of hope.

He tells me the song—the sounds the marks make.

I jump up and down singing it. I shout and laugh like when I was baptized in the creek. I have jumped into another world and I am saved.

But I have to know more. "Tell me more," I say.

"What's your name?" he asks.

"Booker," I say.

And he takes the sound of my name and draws it on the ground.

I linger over that picture. I know I can hold it forever.